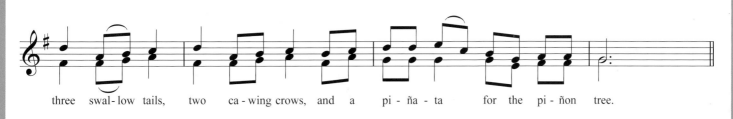

three swal-low tails, two ca-wing crows, and a pi-ña-ta for the pi-ñon tree.

On the fifth day of Christ-mas mis a-migos brought to me: five sil - ver beads,

four nes-ting doves, three swal-low tails, two ca-wing crows, and a pi-ña-ta for the pi-ñon tree.

(repeat as necessary)

On the sixth day of Christ-mas mis a-migos brought to me: six poin-set-tias bloo-min', five sil - ver beads,
On the seventh day...
etc.

four nes-ting doves, three swal-low tails, two ca-wing crows, and a pi-ña-ta for the pi-ñon tree.

THE TWELVE DAYS OF CHRISTMAS

A PIÑATA FOR THE PIÑON TREE

by **Philemon Sturges**

Illustrated by **Ashley Wolff**

LITTLE, BROWN AND COMPANY
New York ⁓ Boston

Also by Philemon Sturges and illustrated by Ashley Wolff:

Who Took the Cookies from the Cookie Jar?
(with Bonnie Lass)
She'll Be Comin' 'Round the Mountain

Also illustrated by Ashley Wolff:

Home to Me, Home to You
Los Pollitos Dicen/The Baby Chicks Are Singing
Oh, the Colors/ De Colores

**To two of Philemon's favorite people: Ashley and Ursula
—Philemon and Judy Sue**

For Judy Sue, and in loving memory of Philemon Sturges,
whose life was the best gift of all. —A.W.

Text copyright © 2007 by Philemon Sturges
Illustrations copyright © 2007 by Ashley Wolff

Little, Brown and Company

Hachette Book Group USA
237 Park Avenue, New York, NY 10017
Visit our Web site at www.lb-kids.com

First Edition: October 2007

ISBN-13: 978-0-316-82323-4
ISBN-10: 0-316-82323-6

10 9 8 7 6 5 4 3 2 1

TWP

Printed in Singapore

The illustrations for this book were done in gouache and pastel on Arches Cover paper.

The text was set in Obelisk, and the display type is Juanita Xilo.

On the first day of Christmas
mis amigos brought to me:

a piñata for the piñon tree.

Bizcochitos

This state cookie can be found in every
New Mexican home at Christmastime.

...ks) unsalted butter

1 teaspoon baking powder

On the second day of Christmas
mis amigos brought to me:

two cawing crows
and a piñata for the piñon tree.

On the third day of Christmas
mis amigos brought to me:

three swallowtails
two cawing crows
and a piñata for the piñon tree.

On the fourth day of Christmas
mis amigos brought to me:

four nesting doves
three swallowtails
two cawing crows
and a piñata for the piñon tree.

On the fifth day of Christmas
mis amigos brought to me:

five silver beads
four nesting doves
three swallowtails
two cawing crows
and a piñata for the piñon tree.

On the sixth day of Christmas
mis amigos brought to me:

six poinsettias bloomin'
five silver beads
four nesting doves
three swallowtails
two cawing crows
and a piñata for the piñon tree.

ANISEED

On the seventh day of Christmas
mis amigos brought to me:

seven skinks a-skulking
six poinsettias bloomin'
five silver beads
four nesting doves
three swallowtails
two cawing crows
and a piñata for the piñon tree.

On the eighth day of Christmas
mis amigos brought to me:

eight coyotes yowlin'
seven skinks a-skulking
six poinsettias bloomin'
five silver beads
four nesting doves
three swallowtails
two cawing crows
and a piñata for the piñon tree.

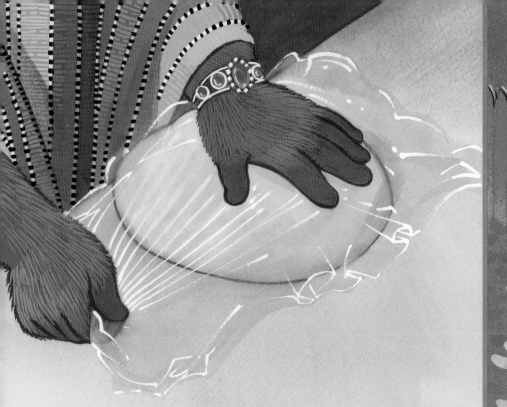

On the ninth day of Christmas
mis amigos brought to me:

nine cowgirls yodelin'
eight coyotes yowlin'
seven skinks a-skulking
six poinsettias bloomin'
five silver beads
four nesting doves
three swallowtails
two cawing crows
and a piñata for the piñon tree.

and a piñata for the piñon tree!

On the tenth day of Christmas
mis amigos brought to me:

ten kachina leapin'
nine cowgirls yodelin'
eight coyotes yowlin'
seven skinks a-skulking
six poinsettias bloomin'
five silver beads
four nesting doves
three swallowtails
two cawing crows
and a piñata for the piñon tree.

On the eleventh day of Christmas
mis amigos brought to me:

eleven mariachi
ten kachina leapin'
nine cowgirls yodelin'
eight coyotes yowlin'
seven skinks a-skulking,
six poinsettias bloomin'
five silver beads
four nesting doves
three swallowtails
two cawing crows
and a piñata for the piñon tree.

On the twelfth day of Christmas
mis amigos brought to me:

twelve drummers drumming
eleven mariachi
ten kachina leapin'
nine cowgirls yodelin'
eight coyotes yowlin'
seven skinks a-skulking
six poinsettias bloomin'
five silver beads
four nesting doves
three swallowtails
two cawing crows

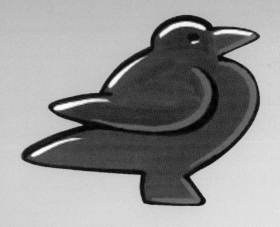

Bizcochitos

This state cookie can be found in every New Mexican home at Christmastime.

1 cup (2 sticks) unsalted butter
1 1/2 cups sugar
3 1/2 cups flour
1 teaspoon baking powder
1 tablespoon aniseed
3 large eggs
1/2 teaspoon vanilla extract
1 teaspoon lemon zest

In a mixing bowl, cream together the butter and sugar until smooth. In a separate bowl, sift together the flour and baking powder and add the aniseed.

Gradually add the dry ingredients to the butter-sugar mixture and combine well. Add the eggs, vanilla, and lemon zest, and mix until the dough is smooth. Cover the dough with plastic wrap and chill for two hours in the refrigerator.